To
Don and Mary MacKinnon
for
enriching my life

Thanks
to
Glenn Keator, Ph.D.
Director of Education
Strybing Arboretum Society
San Francisco, California
and the
Helen Crocker Russel Horticultural Library

Reinforced binding of hardcover edition suitable for library use.

Copyright © 1984 by Ruth Heller.
All rights reserved. Published by Grosset & Dunlap, Inc.,
a member of The Putnam & Grosset Book Group, New York.
Published simultaneously in Canada. Sandcastle Books and the Sandcastle logo
are trademarks belonging to The Putnam & Grosset Book Group.
First Sandcastle Books edition, 1992. Printed in Singapore.
Library of Congress Catalog Card Number: 84-80502
ISBN (hardcover) 0-448-18964-X   F G H I J
ISBN (Sandcastle) 0-448-41092-3   C D E F G H I J

PLANTS THAT NEVER EVER BLOOM

Written and Illustrated by
RUTH HELLER

GROSSET & DUNLAP, NEW YORK

A MUSHROOM
doesn't ever
bloom.

It grows
on trees
and leaves
and things…

or
in the grass
in
fairy
rings.

Some grow to be…

as tall as all
of these you see,

and some
look
rather
strange
to me.

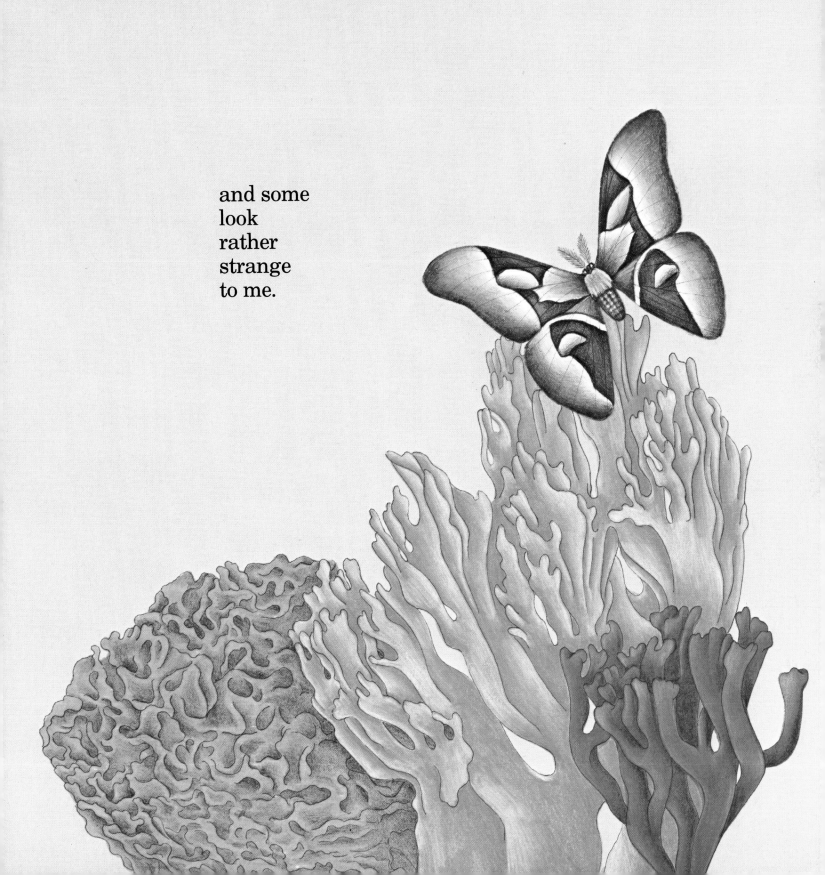

These glow at night.
We don't know why.

MUSHROOMS
all
are
called
FUNGI.

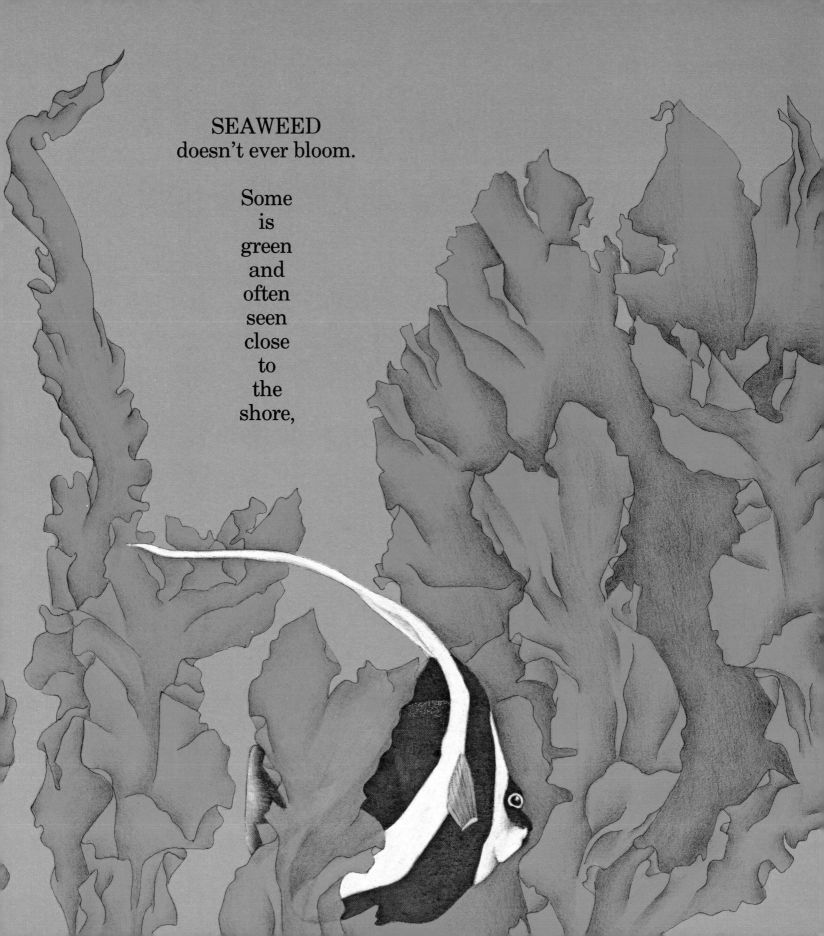

SEAWEED
doesn't ever bloom.

Some
is
green
and
often
seen
close
to
the
shore,

but
there
is
more…

deeper down
where it is
several shades of brown.

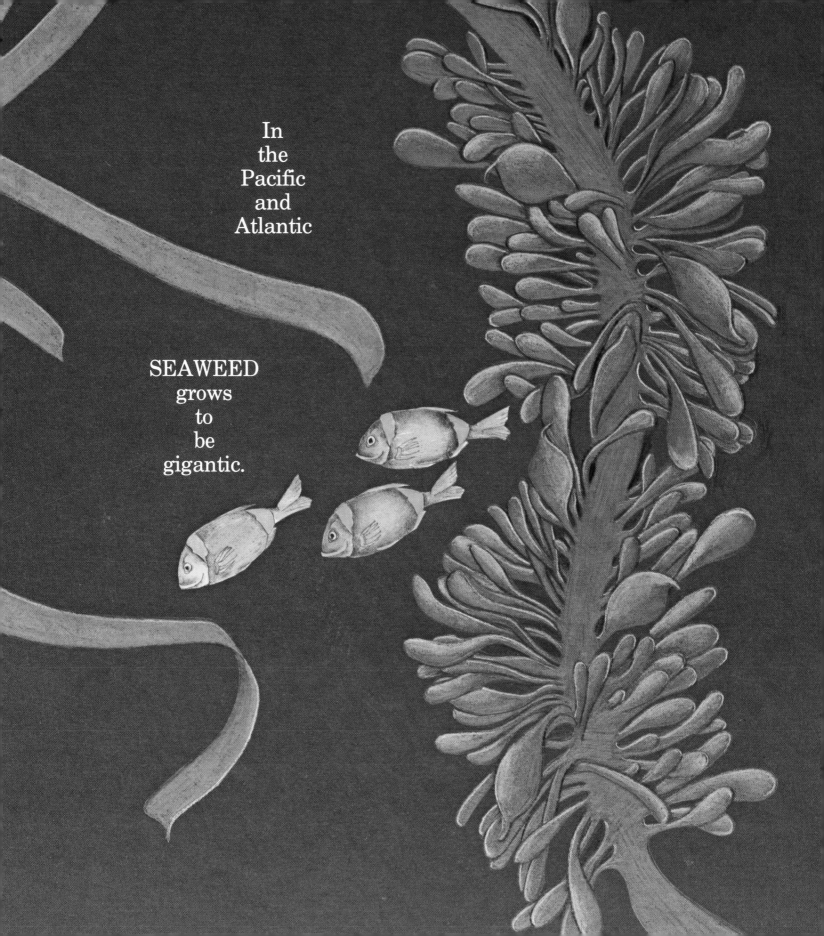

In
the
Pacific
and
Atlantic

SEAWEED
grows
to
be
gigantic.

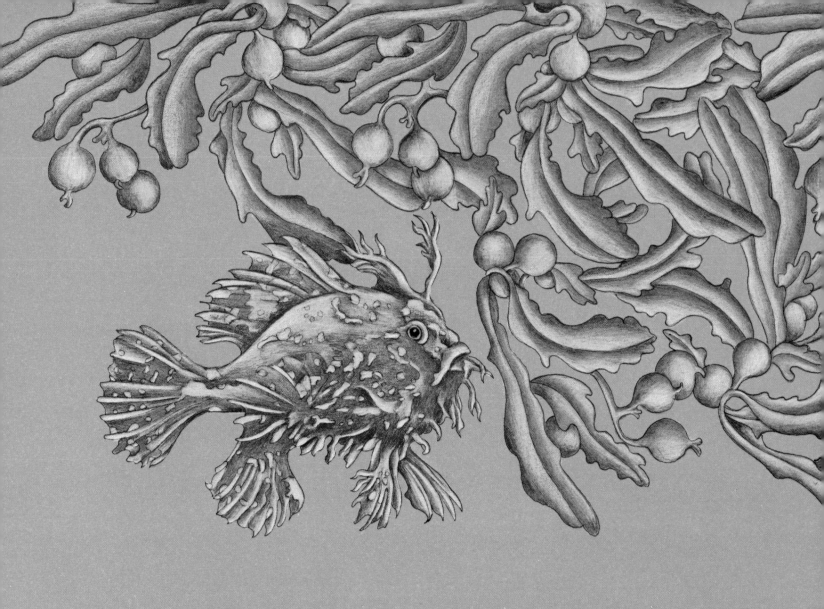

This mass has broken free
and floats in the
Sargasso Sea
where grumpy-looking fish reside…

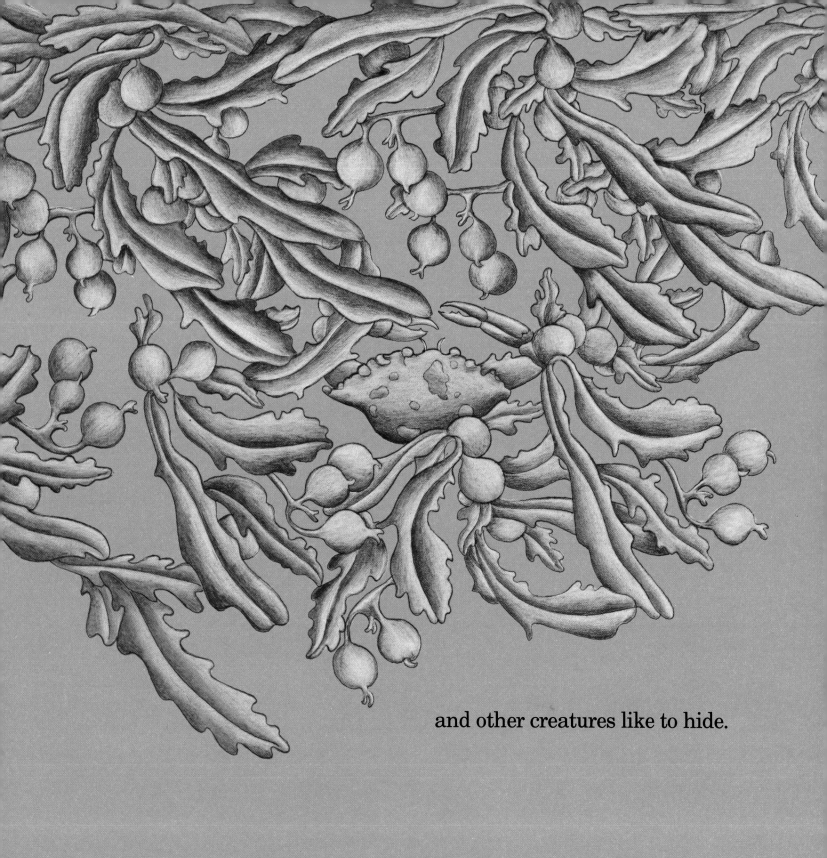

and other creatures like to hide.

Deepest on the
ocean bed
is
SEAWEED
that is
pink
and
red.

Whichever
color it may be
SEAWEED
all is called
ALGAE.

LICHEN never ever blooms.
It lives on logs
and trees
and rocks,

and
sometimes
grows
on
little
stalks.

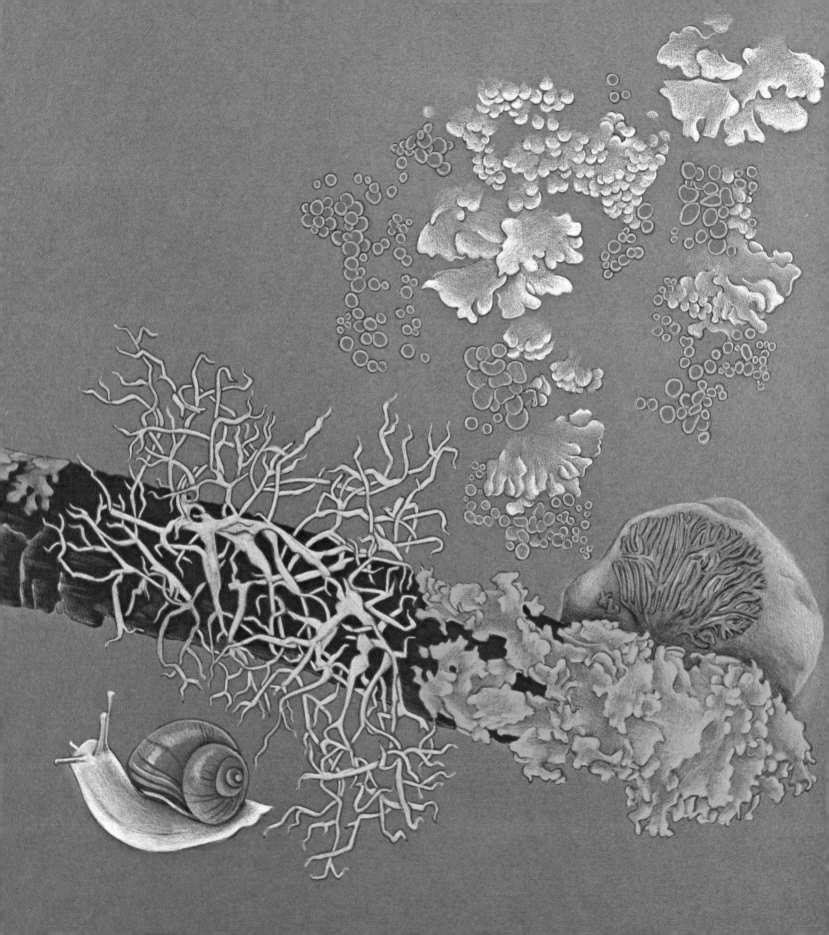

Lush
MOSS

that
clings
to trees...

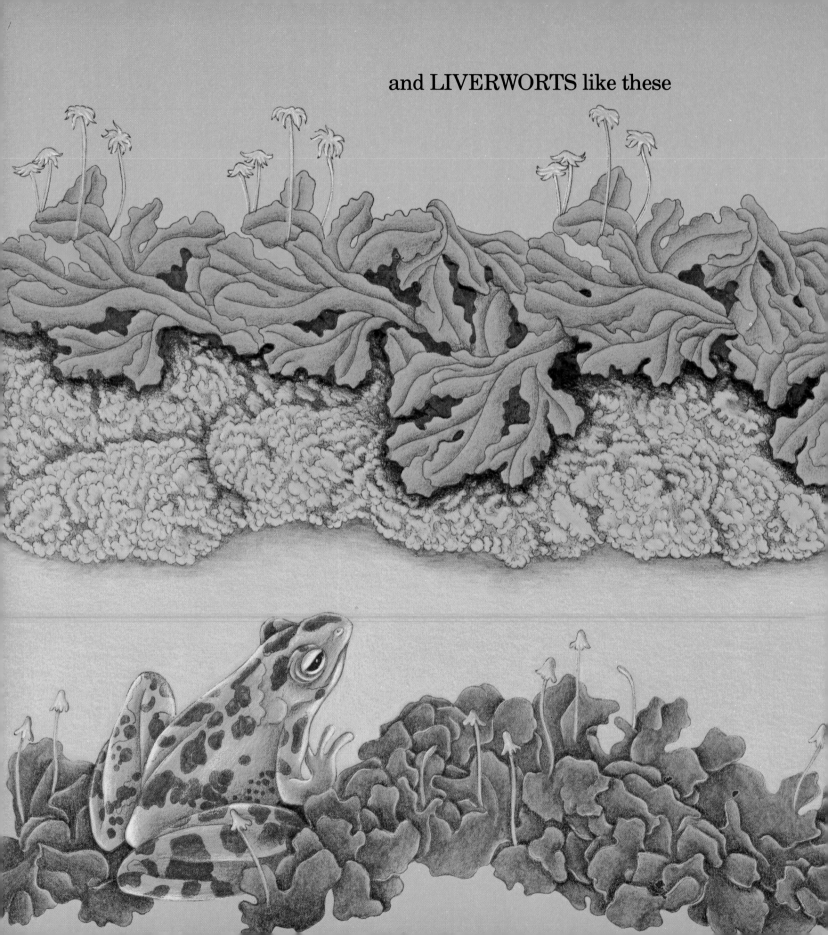

and LIVERWORTS like these

that grow beside a stream are green,

but not a
flower
can be seen.

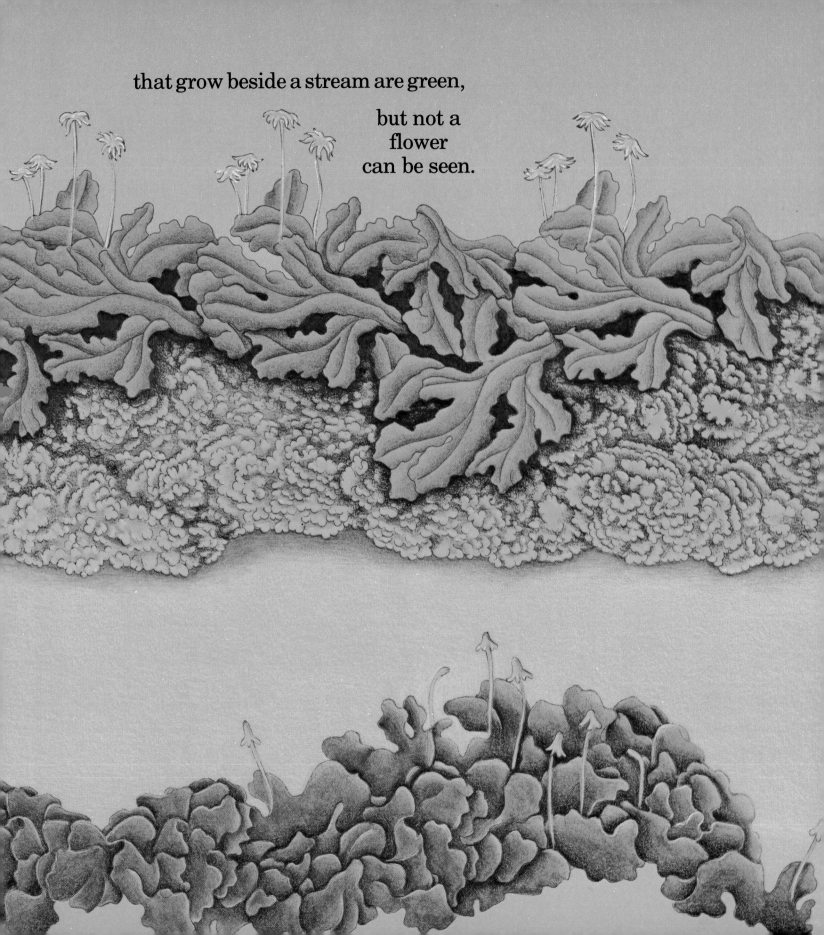

FERNS…

from
fiddleheads
unfurl.

Their
cousins
are
the
HORSETAILS

and
this
creeping
evergreen,

and not on any one of these
are flowers ever seen.

Two hundred million years ago
FERNS
were rather small.

Their cousins,
on the other hand,
grew
very,
very
tall.

None of these
have flowers,
and so
they have
no seeds.

They have no seeds,
as I have said,
they grow from
tiny SPORES instead.

But here are some exceptions. There always are a few.

Like
all
the
rest

they
never
bloom

but
from
a
seed
they
grew.

One
is
called
the
GINKGO,

another
is
the
YEW....

And
every
plant
that
bears
a
CONE

is
an
exception
too.

In
proper
scientific
terms
all
of
these
are
GYM·NO·SPERMS·